A Morning to Polish and Keep

"AMY! TIME TO GET UP!"

A Morning to Polish and Keep

Story by JULIE LAWSON
Illustrations by SHEENA LOTT

NORTHERN LIGHTS BOOKS FOR CHILDREN

Red Deer College Press

Northern Lights Books for Children are published by
Red Deer College Press
56 Avenue & 32 Street Box 5005
Red Deer Alberta Canada T4N 5H5

Acknowledgements
Edited for the Press by Tim Wynne-Jones.
Design by Dennis Johnson.
Printed and bound in Canada by Friesens for Red Deer College Press.
Financial support provided by the Alberta Foundation for the Arts, a
beneficiary of the Lottery Fund of the Government of Alberta, and by
the Canada Council, the Department of Communications and Red
Deer College.

First paperback edition 1998.   5 4 3 2 1

Canadian Cataloguing in Publication Data
Lawson, Julie, 1947–
A morning to polish and keep
(Northern lights books for children)
ISBN 0-88995-082-2 (bound) — ISBN 0-88995-179-9 (pbk.)
I. Lott, Sheena, 1950–   II. Title
PS8573.A94M67 1992   jC813'.54   C91-091845-7
PR9199.3.L3395M67 1992

COMMITTED TO THE DEVELOPMENT OF CULTURE AND THE ARTS

THE CANADA COUNCIL | LE CONSEIL DES ARTS
FOR THE ARTS | DU CANADA
SINCE 1957 | DEPUIS 1957

*T*o my Dad, Charles (Chuck) Goodwin…for all the happy summers.
–Julie Lawson

*T*o my Mother and Father.
–Sheena Lott

We left the cabin under a still-starlit sky: Mom, Dad, Michael and me. In single file we followed the path across the salt marsh, our footprints glistening in the dew. My first time up before dawn!

"It's like we're the only people in the world!" I whispered as we crossed the wooden bridge over the slough.

At the edge of the marsh, we crunched along the beach, over pebbles, barnacles and broken shells. Slippery seaweed squished beneath our feet. My nose wrinkled with the clammy reek of low tide.

We stepped carefully along the creaking planks of the wharf. The tide was out so far the boat was barely floating.

"Take it easy," Mom said as we clambered aboard.

Dad started the engine. It sputtered and coughed, then eased into a smooth running hum.

The boat sped along the sleeping shoreline of the Basin, spinning a trail of quicksilver. It skimmed through the mouth of the river, into the harbor and around the spit that stretched its long finger into the sea. The passage was tricky—especially against the pull of the tide. Dad guided the boat carefully round the point, and then we zoomed into the Strait.

"See that island?" Dad said. "That's the Island of Second Chances. That's where I lost the big one last week. Maybe he's still around!"

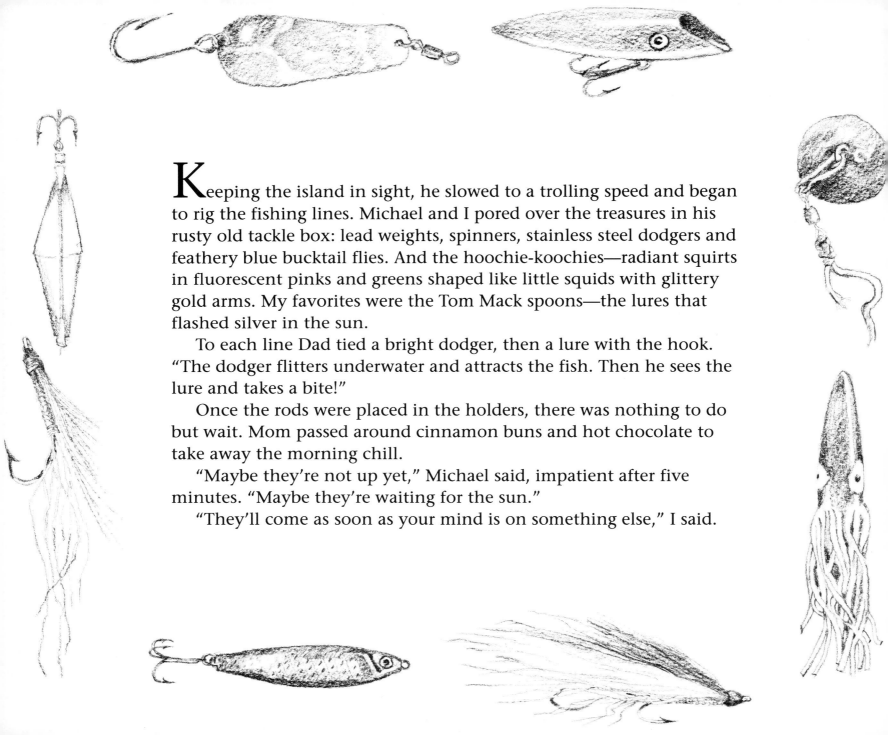

Keeping the island in sight, he slowed to a trolling speed and began to rig the fishing lines. Michael and I pored over the treasures in his rusty old tackle box: lead weights, spinners, stainless steel dodgers and feathery blue bucktail flies. And the hoochie-koochies—radiant squirts in fluorescent pinks and greens shaped like little squids with glittery gold arms. My favorites were the Tom Mack spoons—the lures that flashed silver in the sun.

To each line Dad tied a bright dodger, then a lure with the hook. "The dodger flitters underwater and attracts the fish. Then he sees the lure and takes a bite!"

Once the rods were placed in the holders, there was nothing to do but wait. Mom passed around cinnamon buns and hot chocolate to take away the morning chill.

"Maybe they're not up yet," Michael said, impatient after five minutes. "Maybe they're waiting for the sun."

"They'll come as soon as your mind is on something else," I said.

Except for some skylighting seagulls, we were the only living things on the water. But beneath the surface was a whole other world teeming with life. Salmon were making one last sweep of the sea before heading upriver. Spiny-finned rockfish darted in and out of the kelp beds. Moon jellyfish floated like parachutes through the currents.

I imagined a mermaid drifting in and out of the deep sea shadows, playing hide and seek with a golden seal or waiting to catch a glimpse of the sun.

Gradually the sky became lighter. Darkness crept away little by little, turning our world to pale shades of blue and misty gray. Then suddenly—the sky was on fire! We were caught in the blaze of sunrise. Dad looked at his watch. "Right on schedule," he said.

But it was another hour before the fish paid any attention to our hooks and lines. That's the way it is with fishing. Nothing happens for such a long time, and then when you least expect it …

"You've got one! A big one!" Everyone was yelling at once. "Atta girl, Amy! Hang on! Don't lose him! You want some help?"

"No, no!" I cried. "I can do it!"

"Easy, easy," Dad said. "Let the line out a bit…. Give it some slack … then reel in…. That's right…."

Oh, he was a big one! And such a fighter! The rod rammed into my chest, my heart pounded, my arms ached, my eyes prickled from the sunlight glinting off the water. But I wouldn't give up.

"He must be a coho! He's *huge!* Keep going.... You've almost got him!"

Dad had the net ready and was leaning over to scoop him out of the water when Michael suddenly cried, "Look! Killer whales!"

In that split second, I lost my grip. The rod leaped out of my hands. It was gone, just like that—hook, line and sinker. And my salmon with it.

"Michael!" I yelled.

"Never mind," said Dad, patting my shoulder.

I broke away to the other side of the boat and stared fixedly at the water.

"Look at the whales, Amy," said Mom. "In all the times your father and I've been out here, we've never seen them. Not once."

"Must be a present for you kids," said Dad.

The shoreline swam in and out of focus through my tears.

"Look, Amy!" Michael said. "There's three, four, *five!* They're getting closer!"

In my mind I could see them leaping, splashing and slapping their tails. But I wouldn't look.

Then, through the corner of my eye, I caught a glimpse…. And blinking back the tears, I turned to the wonder of the whales. Soon they were alongside our boat, and we felt the cool spray of their passing as they streamed on up the coast.

"A lucky sign," said Mom.

"I'll drink to that!" exclaimed Dad, pouring himself more hot chocolate. "Anybody else?"

We sat quietly, sipping our drinks and finishing the cinnamon buns. But the whales were gone, and my rod was gone and I still felt empty inside.

"Don't feel bad, Amy," said Michael. "It's the Island of Second Chances, remember?"

I glared at him. What good was a second chance when I didn't even have my fishing rod?

Bit by bit the morning unfolded, getting warmer and brighter as the sun rose. By now other boats were on the water, fishing lines were arched, poised and ready, waiting … waiting …

Then it came again. A whopping great THUMP, THUMP, THUMP and Michael's line pounding against the edge of the boat.

"I've got it!" he cried.

Dad gritted his teeth, itching to get his hands on the rod to make sure *this* one wouldn't get away. I gritted my teeth, too.

"I can do it myself!" Michael said.

I clenched my fists and bit my lip. I could see him getting tired. Suddenly, the line sped out with a ghastly whir!

"Hang on!" I spun to his side. "Turn the reel…. Come on…. Keep going! Now let the line out a bit so it won't snap," I coached. "That's it…. Now reel it in…. You can do it!"

It was such a struggle for him. But he kept straining away, determined to bring in that fish. Then we saw it.

"**Y**ou've caught Amy's fishing rod!" said Mom.

Sure enough, it was my rod. Somehow that fish had got tangled up in the line and Michael was reeling it *all* in—hook, line, sinker *and* salmon.

"I'll be a tickled herring!" said Dad.

"Take it, Amy," said Michael. He was practically out of breath. "He's your fish."

I swallowed hard. "I'll just give you a hand," I said, and we reeled it in together.

Dad was right there with the net, and this time there were no distractions. We were having fresh salmon for supper.

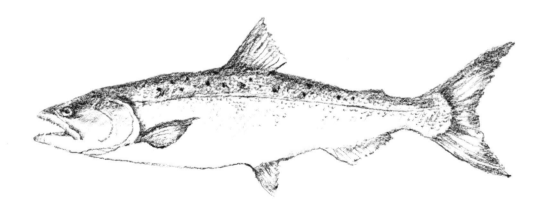

"Well," said Dad as we put away the tackle, "you've got quite a fish story to tell."

"A real one, too!" said Mom. She winked at me. "For once it's not about the one that got away."

I picked a small silver lure out of the tackle box. "Can I have this?"

"Sure," said Dad. He was about to remove the hook, but I stopped him. "I'll be careful." Dad and Mom looked at each other. "The hook is part of the morning," I said.

After a moment they both nodded. Dad handed me the lure, hook and all. "I'll put it on my hat the way fishermen do," I said.

"How about you, Michael?" said Dad. "You want a souvenir, too?"

"Yeah—the whole tackle box!" he said.

Michael and I took turns steering the boat on the way back. It was like riding into the heart of a jewel, everything was so sun-struck, sharp and sparkly. I imagined the mermaid playing in our wake, catching rainbows in the spray.

In the wind I could feel the bite of autumn. Soon the river would be alive with salmon making their way upstream to spawn. Tomorrow we would close up the cabin and go back to the city.

"That's it, then," Dad said, reading my thoughts. "Another summer gone."

"Not for me," I said, holding up the silver lure. "I'm keeping it in here!"

Dad and Mom and Michael smiled. And I put all their smiles in it as well.

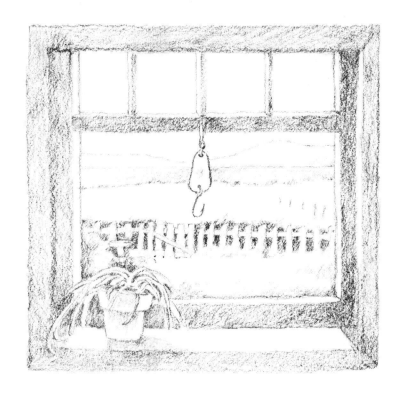

That silver lure now hangs in my window, ready to bring back a memory of summer. Of all the mornings I've known since then, that's the one I take out most often for another look. It's a bit hazy around the edges, but when I give it a polish it comes out bright and clear and shining.